李達

惠存

張山 2020

終極

陶陣

Ultimate Ceramic Arrays

張山 創作展 CHANG Shan

109年苗栗縣美術家邀請展

目錄
CONTENTS

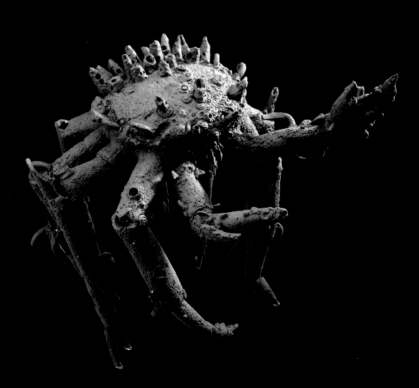

作品
ARTWORK

縣長 序

　　坐落中部的苗栗縣東倚雪山山脈，西濱台灣海峽，擁有豐富的高山森林，溪河海岸的自然美景，聚落在此的人們，發展出在地自然共生、純樸宜居、共融慢活的風土民情，也蘊育出多位不凡的藝術創作家。本縣為提昇在地文化品味，多年對於推廣在地文化與藝術創作不遺餘力，期許結合人文與經濟，帶動幸福山城的藝文產業發展。

　　鍾靈毓秀，人文薈萃的山城苗栗，多少藝術家在此陶冶性情，創作作品。為提昇苗栗縣的藝術能量，每年苗栗縣政府文化觀光局邀請縣內藝術家辦理個人創作展，表揚嘉獎創作者創作不輟之精神，肯定其藝術之成就，並將巧奪天工的藝術成果精彩呈現，讓藝術美學融入苗栗居民的生活，為苗栗的藝術生態注入豐沛生命力。

　　苗栗擁有優質的陶土與天然瓦斯，在地的苗栗陶創作、柴燒技法更是爐火純青，連年舉辦的苗栗陶藝術節皆吸引陶藝創作的青年才俊皆踴躍參展，帶動苗栗陶藝產業。身為在地創作者的陶藝家張山老師，以獨具特色的風格表現、媒材運用、創作理念，不僅連年獲得國內外獎項殊榮，也致力深耕苗栗在地陶藝文化。張山老師專注創作，作品幾經細心雕琢，不惜多次烈火焚燒，才得塑出剛毅穩健，熠熠生輝的成果。其古意真摯、歷久彌新的陶器上的釉彩，正如山城的一鑑天光雲影，映照出張老師反璞歸真、童心未泯的真性情。

　　「終極陶陣」包羅張山老師各個精彩系列，期許能透過這次展出此股強勁的創作能量，帶起苗栗陶窯藝術的新浪潮。並值本次畫冊成書之際，特為張山老師的創作精神與在地深耕，謹表真摯的謝忱與敬意。

苗栗縣 縣長　徐耀昌

1

Located in central Taiwan, east of the Xueshan Range and west of the Taiwan Strait, Miaoli has magnificent landscapes of tall mountains and rich forests, riverbanks and coasts. People living here are cultivated with a lifestyle that is symbiotic with nature, simple, communal, and slow living. It also breeds many outstanding artists. To promote culture, Miaoli County has promoted local culture and artistic creation with all its efforts, hoping to integrated local humanistic and economic forces to encourage the growth of literary and culture industry in this happy mountain city.

Being a place with genius loci, the mountain city of Miaoli is saturated with humanistic sensations. Many artists are cultivated here, creating brilliant works. To promote the power of artistic creation in Miaoli, the Culture and Tourism Bureau of Miaoli County Government invites local artists to present solo exhibitions every year to promote their dedication to artistic creations and recognize their achievements in art. In addition, we are enthusiastic in presenting their brilliant accomplishments in artistic creation, allowing beauty to merge into the Miaoli people's everyday life. We aspire to inject prolific life forces into Miaoli's ecology of art.

Miaoli has quality clay and natural gas. Local Miaoli ceramic artistic creation and wood-firing techniques are superb. The ceramic art festival held in Miaoli every year attracts many young and fine ceramic artists, promoting Miaoli's ceramic industry. As a local ceramic artist, Mr. Chang Shan won great prizes at home and abroad with his unique styles, usage of media, and sophisticated ideal in artistic creation. He also dedicated himself deeply to promote local ceramic art culture in Miaoli. Focusing on artistic creation, his works are well-wrought. Fired repeatedly, his works begin to show sturdiness and stableness, displaying brilliant achievements. Being cute and true, the color glazes of his works are long lasting, like the skylight and clouds' colors in the mountain city. It reflects Chang Shan's return to innocence and his truthfulness of a child's heart.

"Ultimate Ceramic Arrays" include many of Chang Shan's exciting works. I sincerely expected him to promote new waves in ceramic art creation in Miaoli with his momentous power in artistic creation. With the publishing of the album, I would like to express my sincere gratitude to Chang Shan's enthusiasm in artistic creation and his dedications in cultivating local art.

Hsu, Yao-chang
Magistrate of Miaoli County

局長序
Preface by the Director

　　苗栗縣政府文化觀光局將推動苗栗藝文發展爲己任，每年透過歸廣辦理各種文教展演及藝文節慶活動，提昇苗栗縣藝術文化品質、整合藝術文化產業資源，以達到培養觀眾欣賞藝文活動習慣，增進在地居民文化素質，鼓勵當地藝術創作者持續創作之目標。

　　自 97 年起「苗栗縣美術家邀請展」公開辦理至今，不論媒材運用、風格技法、創作議題，各種精彩的作品登台亮相，不僅爲肯定苗栗縣美術創作者的舞台，更支持本縣之美術創作、提昇苗栗的美術創作能量、拔擢美術創作人才。苗栗山城的文化底蘊，加上豐沛的美術創作能量，不僅給予了創作者廣大的靈感，也爲觀展民眾帶來藝術層面的內心啓發與探討。

　　本年度展覽邀請之陶藝創作家－張山先生，1960 年生於台灣苗栗銅鑼，是一位賦予公仔陶偶嶄新生命，具有強烈個人色彩的陶藝創作家。善於將陶土的表面肌理燒製成鐵鏽質感，表現出滄海桑田的光陰痕跡，帶給觀者對於歲月的反思。爲了塑造每個作品的獨特性，公仔卡通人物更以局部噴彩、傳統圖騰、表情細節等技法重新解構詮釋，展現出不同個性與情緒的張力。除了將充滿玩趣的公仔陶偶作爲主題之外，以海洋生物作爲創作主題的海洋系列，透過鏽蝕表皮呈現的海洋生物，使人深刻反思海洋生態與人類文明的拉鋸矛盾。本次展覽以「終極陶陣」爲題，藉由兵列陣法的形式引導觀者探索作者無遠弗屆的想像力以及濃烈渾厚的創作理念。

　　鐵與陶，工業與自然，乍看突兀相斥的元素，卻在張山先生的創作中共融成充滿趣味又使人反思的底蘊。習慣了現代化都市的我們，也在張山先生的作品中重溫到陶土的溫度。苗栗山城，在繁華的寶島中部作爲銜接都會之間的綠洲，除了坐擁豐美的山林溪河，更是保有珍貴的人文內涵，期許能藉著每年實踐創作展演、藝術休閒的活動，加強在地創作者之互動與交流，並持續帶動苗栗的文化能量，在苗栗這塊豐饒的土地上，蘊育出文化的果實。

苗栗縣政府文化觀光局 局長　林彥甫

The Culture and Tourism Bureau of Miaoli County Government regards the promotion of the development of literature and art as its mission. Each year, it sponsors various literary and educational exhibitions and literary and art festivals to elevate the literary and art quality of Miaoli County and integrate art and cultural industry. Cultivating audiences' habits of enjoying literary and art activities, it aims to promote local residents' cultural literacy and encourage locate artists to continue creating arts.

Since 2008, the "Miaoli County Artists Invitation Exhibition" has been conducted each year. Regarding the use of media, styles, techniques, and issues of creation are conveyed in the works displayed. It not only endorses the stage for creative artists in Miaoli, but also supports the power and enhances the momentum of artistic creation in Miaoli, cultivating more talents. With the cultural essence in Miaoli and the ample energy in artistic creation, it gives creative artists plenty of inspirations and brings people inspirations at heart, encouraging them to explore art further.

The artist invited in the exhibition this year is Mr. Chang Shan. Born in 1960 in Tong Luo, Miaoli, he is an artist and a color ceramic artist with a strong personal style that animates dolls. Skillful in processing the surface texture of clay and fire it into the quality of iron rust, his works express the traces and changes of time, inviting audiences to ponder the issues of time. To construct the uniqueness of each work, the cartoon figures use various techniques, such as partially sprayed color, painted traditional totems, and engraved nuance of expressions to reinterpret materials deconstructively, demonstrating different personalities and emotional tension. In addition to using interesting ceramic dolls as themes, Chang also uses marine creatures as themes for creation in his ocean series. Presenting marine creatures with rusty surfaces, he invites people to ponder the paradox of the marine ecology and human civilization. Titled "Ultimate Ceramic Arrays", this exhibition uses military arrays to guide the audience to explore the artist's infinite imagination, strong and solid creative ideals.

Iron and ceramic, industry and nature, seem to be paradoxical elements. Nevertheless, they blend into each other seamlessly in Chang Shan's works, provoking interesting and profound thoughts. Accustomed to the urban lifestyle, we can re-feel the warmth in his works. Miaoli, the mountain city in central Taiwan, is an oasis connecting the prosperous capitals. Embracing beautiful mountains and rivers, it retains the precious essence of the humanities. It aspires to achieve the goals of sponsoring exhibitions for creative arts and leisure and art activities every year to promote exchanges among creative artists and continue to promote Miaoli's cultural power and breed ample fruits of culture on the fertile soil of Miaoli.

Lin Yen-fu
Director of Culture and Tourism Bureau, Miaoli County

不被拘束的想法、勇於嘗試的創新

　　認識張山大哥是在 2009 年台北陶藝獎時，記得當年他得了創新組首獎，初次見面，因為聊到都是苗栗人，交流起來，特別有感情！當他介紹他的作品時，很顛覆傳統的創作手法，吸引了我想要多去了解這個作者！

　　他的美術天份有著深厚的底子，不被拘束的想法，勇於嘗試的創新，讓他在創作陶的玩陶路上，更有為之驚艷的作品！

　　「鐵鏽」代表著他的理念與成就…想要傳達對環保議題、海洋污染、動物滅絕…等破壞之因果；美麗的地球，下一代的未來，希望這一代人能好好愛護，傳承！

　　也因這份特殊，讓他榮獲許多大獎，讓大眾正視此議題！

　　近年來，張山大哥轉往「公仔」路線，這是個現代的流行，各式各樣的公仔是百年來陶瓷都存在著的產品，但是加以「鐵鏽」理念，讓公仔作品有了性格表徵，有了故事…調皮、暴力、憤怒、都是表達著張山大哥人生不同歷練的紀錄！

　　認識了十幾年…你說他厲害嗎～

　　我覺得，看過他的作品，品嚐過內容，不得不佩服，玩陶，能玩得自我、玩得不被拘束、讓陶賦予生命力，讓欣賞者感受到他充滿故事的人生，這是會讓人覺得親切且會心一笑的

苗栗縣山城藝術文化協會 理事長 張 國 森

Without being harnessed by traditional thinking, daring to make innovations

I came to know Mr. Chang Shan at the Taipei Ceramics Awards in 2009. I remembered that he won first prize in the innovation category. When I first met him, I learned that he was also from Miaoli in our chat. We both felt the affections of folks between us during our exchange. When he introduced his works, he used subversive techniques in his creation. It attracted me to know this artist more.

He was profoundly trained and talented in art, without being harnessed by traditional thinking. He dared to make innovation, allowing him to create amazing works in the creation of toying with ceramic art.

"Iron rust" represented his ideal and achievements. He wanted to show the causes and results of damage in the issues of environmental protection, ocean pollution, animal extinction, etc. He hoped people of this generation would love the earth and hand the beautiful planet to the next generation. Because of this special style, he won many prestigious prizes, alerting people to face these issues.

In recent years, Chang shifted to the creation of "dolls", his latest trend. Dolls with different styles and looks are existing features of ceramic art in the past one hundred years. But presenting them with the ideal of "iron rust", it animates them with personalities. There are naughty, violent, and angry stories, recording Chang Shan's experiences in different stage of life.

I have known him for more than a decade. If we say he is superb, we have to agree without any question, after seeing his works and pondering upon the contents. He finds himself in crafting and toying with ceramic art without any restraint. He gives life to ceramic art, allowing people to feel his life story. It will make people feel close to him, associated with a hearty smile.

Chang Kuo-sen
Miaoli Mountain City Art and Cultural Association

有種人叫張山，他很複雜！

　　有種人不喜歡在壓力下過生活，有種人覺得自己無法在壓力之下好好的過生活，有種人在沒有壓力的狀態之下覺得自己頂著壓力在過生活，有種人覺得自己應該在可輕鬆承受的壓力狀態之下，過著沒有壓力的生活，有種人叫張山，他很複雜！

　　張山的作品很誠實，反映作者本人的真實樣態，調皮、搞怪、幽默、反骨、悶騷、自戀……，張山的作品不誠實，明明是陶，卻總是喜歡披著鐵、銅、木、石材的外衣，在你遲疑猜測的當下，貌似微笑的公仔用勝利者的姿態鄙視著呆口騷頭的你，而豎眉呲牙咧嘴的傢伙們，卻在猙獰的表情下，迷漫著一股裝模作樣的可愛氣息，這種不誠實的表現手法，誠實地影射了作者的 ” 複雜 ” 人格。

　　陶土被張山玩弄於股掌之間，展現出豐富而多元的面貌，但深入探究，這些仿異材質感的表現手法，顯示出張山對陶瓷這種材料不具備信心，原因來自於陶瓷藝術長久以來被藝術圈邊緣化。相較於木雕、石雕、鑄銅、鐵雕等，陶瓷比較被歸類在工藝領域。這原罪主要在於陶藝的製作需要熟練的技術（不小心會流於炫技），而且，陶瓷在生活實用器上頻繁出現所導致。這種被藝術圈冷處理的無力感，使得張山選擇隱藏陶土本身的質地，運用獨到的騙術默默的衝擊已長久僵化的認知體系，這是自我解嘲也是無聲的抗議！

　　退休後張山老師無須拖著皮囊赴校荼毒幼苗，安逸的日子狀似自在，眼神卻時不時透漏著一絲絲的無所適從與焦躁感。身為後輩的我雖然不是心理醫師，但觀察力還算還算敏銳，我斷言他正處在中年危機！此次的展出表面上嚷嚷著是要回饋故里，並與親朋好友們交流分享，實際上是張山前輩正藉此梳理自我，好似打仗前的裝備保養與心理調適。

　　以上言論純屬個人揣測，是準備棄械投降安養天年還是戰死沙場？讓我們繼續看下去 ……

藝術家 章格銘

A kind of person that called Chang Shan , being complicated.

There is a kind of person that does not like to live under stress. There is also another kind of person that thinks they cannot live well with any pressure. Some people feel they live under stress even if there is not any pressure at all. Some people think they can take stress easily, living a life without any pressure. Chang Shan belongs to the last type, being complicated.

Chang Shan's works are very honest, reflecting the personality of the artist himself, naughty, fancy, humorous, rebellious, showy, narcissistic, etc. Chang Shan's works are not honest. They are ceramic craft in essence but they are always covered with iron, bronze, wood, and stone. When you are guessing hesitatingly, the dolls are teasing you, dumbfounded, in the manner of winners with despair. Those grinning little fellows are hiding their cute personalities under their fearful looking appearances. Such dishonest presentation conveys the artist's "complicated" personality honestly.

The clay is maneuvered by Chang Shan with his skillful fingers, displaying diverse and vivid appearances. Exploring the facts in depth, these imitated materials with the appearances of a false looking quality are a means of presentation. It shows Chang Shan lacks confidence in the material of clay. It is because ceramic art has long been marginalized. Compared with wood carving, stone carving, bronze art, iron carving, etc, ceramic is believed to be a craft, not art. It is because it requires superb artisanship to complete a work (and it will become showy if applying the techniques carelessly). Furthermore, ceramic vessels are used widely in daily life. The feeling of helplessness in the circle of art motivated Chang Shan to conceal the quality of clay. He uses unsurpassed tricky techniques to exert an impact in the cognition system that has been silent and dormant for a long period. It is self-mocking as well as a protest.

Retired, Chang Shan no longer needs to teach children with the identity of a teacher. His easy life seems to be comfortable. But in his eyes, he always shows the anxiety of being uneasy and out of place. As a junior, although I am not a psychiatrist, I am still keen in observation. I can say that he is undergoing a midlife crisis. In this exhibition, in appearance, he claims to return to his hometown and share his art with friends and relatives. Actually, Chang Shan, my senior, is trying to adjust himself psychologically, like maintaining his gear before going to war. These are my personal speculations only.

Is he going to surrender and live a quiet life in the remaining time of his life or go out to combat? Let's wait and see.

Chang Ke-ming
Artist

終極陶陣 - 張山創作展

　　本名張文正，1960 年生於苗栗縣銅鑼鄉，畢業於銅鑼鄉文林國中，國中時期經美術老師的啓蒙，考上新竹師專美術科。1980 年畢業後服務於苗栗縣西湖鄉瑞湖國小。服務五年後，遷調至台北縣泰山國小服務。在校擔任美勞專任教師，當時因北縣教育局推展陶藝教育課程，因而有機會爭取經費，購置陶藝設備，也因此開始了個人陶藝創作的學習。從一個陶藝門外漢，開始參加各類相關課程的學習，並透過設計陶藝教學的過程，邊做邊學，期間參加了無數次的陶藝創作的競賽，獲得了許多佳績。2010 年於新北市新店區北新國小退休。退休後於苗栗縣亞太技術學院擔任駐校藝術家四年。

　　2013 年始成立個人工作室專注於陶藝創作。除了個人創作，同時也積極參與各類的教學、展覽、評審 ... 等活動，爲陶藝的傳承盡一份心力。2020 年初年前獲選苗栗縣文觀局邀請展出，希望藉此機會，就教於前輩與後進。並與鄉親們分享交流。

藝術家 張 山

Ultimate Ceramic Arrays-Ceramics Exhibition of Chang Shan

Chang Shan, originally named Chang Wen-cheng, was born in Tongluo, Miaoli in 1960. Graduating from Wenlin Junior High School in Tongluo Township, he passed the examination and entered the Department of Art, Hsinchu Teacher's College because of the inspiration of his junior high school art teacher. He graduated in 1980 and began to teach at Ruihu Elementary School in Xihu Township, Miaoli County. Teaching for five years, he was transferred to Taishan Elementary School in Taipei County and worked as a full-time art teacher. As the Department of Education of Taipei County promoted ceramic art education at that time, I had the opportunity to secure funds to purchase ceramic craft facilities. Likewise, I began to learn the craft of ceramic art. As a layperson in ceramic art, I began to take related lessons. During the ceramic design and art lessons, I practiced what I had learned from the classes. In that period, I participated in many ceramic art contests, winning plenty of awards. In 2010, I retired from Beixin Elementary School in Xindian, New Taipei City. After retirement, I worked as an artist-in-residence at the Asia-Pacific Institute of Creativity, Miaoli County, for four years.

In 2013, I established my personal studio and dedicated myself to ceramic art creation. In addition to my own artistic creation, I was also active in teaching, exhibiting my works, acting as a judge, etc, to contribute my efforts in ceramic art. In early 2020, I was invited to exhibit my works by the Culture and Tourism Bureau, Miaoli County after a demanding screening. I would like to take this opportunity to exchange ideas with younger and elder artists and share my art with folks in Miaoli.

Chang Shan
Artist

作者簡歷

本土陶藝創作家張山，1960年生於台灣苗栗銅鑼。

　　或許是身為一個美術老師的經歷，在從事三十年的陶藝創作歷程中，他的作品中滿溢著濃濃的赤子之心，將自己天馬行空的想法，結合精湛的陶藝材質技巧，捏塑出濃烈風格的藝術創作。其中，在陶藝創作時使用特別的燒製技法，表現出鐵鏽感的表面肌理，正是張山最為人看過一次便過目不忘的個人代表特色。張山自我剖析：「鐵製物充斥在我們當代的生活中，而隨著歲月留下氧化鏽蝕的痕跡，宛如一種生命的消長，時光的輪迴，我對鏽蝕質感，總有特別的觸動」在本展，觀客不妨細細品味每一件展品透過鏽蝕的痕跡與氧化的質感展現的歲月光輝，從中感受陶與鐵的衝突，現代造物與遠古質感的火花。

Artist's Bio

　　Chang Shan, a local ceramic artist, was born in Tongluo, Miaoli, Taiwan in 1960.

　　Perhaps because he was an art teacher, the experience allowed him to create art with a child's heart during his career of ceramic art creation over the past three decades. With unrestrained imagination, he uses superb techniques in handling ceramic art. He plasters his artworks with a strong personal style. In his ceramic art creation, he uses special techniques to create rusty textures on the surfaces of his works. This is a personal style that impresses people deeply at a glance. Chang Shan explains his art, "Iron objects are abundant in our daily life. In the course of time, they become rusty due to oxidization. Like the waxing and waning of life and the wheel of time, I have special feelings towards the rusty quality." In this exhibition, audience members are recommended to observe the glory of time manifested through the traces of rust and the quality of oxidization to feel the conflicts of ceramic and iron, and the sparkles triggered off between antiques and modern objects.

1960 張文正（張山）苗栗 台灣
1980 新竹師專美術科，新竹 台灣
1995 學士，台北市立師範學院，台北 台灣
1980-2010 國小教師，台北 台灣
2010-2015 駐校藝術家，亞太創意技術學院，苗栗 台灣
2017 第 22 屆新竹教育大學傑出校友

展覽：
2006 亞細亞陶藝三角洲（台日韓三國巡迴展）聯展 歧阜 日本
2007 台北縣鶯歌陶瓷博物館 回收場記事 個展 台北 台灣
2007 台北藝術大學—關渡美術館 海洋牧場 個展 台北 台灣
2008 北京奧運文化節 < 藝器 造藝 >
　　台灣當代陶藝展 北京 / 中國美術館 聯展
2008 海洋記事 陶華灼藝廊 台北鶯歌 個展
2011 台灣當代陶藝展 石頭 功夫 仔 個展 苗栗 台灣
2014 中藝博國際畫廊博覽會 北京國家會議中心 北京 中國
2015 高雄藝術博覽會 聯展 高雄 台灣
2015 福爾摩沙藝術博覽會 聯展 台中 台灣
2016 雲清藝術中心 - 虛實之間 聯展 台北 台灣
2016 不可愛聯盟 個展 大河美術 苗栗 台灣

得獎：
2008 台灣國際陶藝年展 評審推薦獎
2008 苗栗陶藝競賽 第一名
2009 第六屆台北陶藝獎創新組 首獎
2009 彰化縣第十屆磺溪獎立體工藝類 磺溪獎
2009 第二屆台灣金壺獎設計競賽 銀獎
2009 苗栗陶藝競賽 優選
2010 台南南瀛雙年展 南瀛獎
2011 第三屆台灣金壺獎設計競賽 銀獎
2012 台北國際陶藝雙年展 入選
2013 第四屆台灣金壺獎設計競賽 佳作
2016 國際茶席美學設計大賽 鶯歌陶瓷博物館 最佳創新獎

1960 Chang Wen-cheng (Chang Shan) Miaoli, Taiwan
1980 Graduated from the Department of Art, Hsinchu Junior College of Education, Hsinchu, Taiwan
1995 BA, Municipal Taipei College of Education, Taiwan
1980-2010 Elementary School Teacher, Taipei, Taiwan
2010-2015 Artist-in-Residence, Asia-Pacific Institute of Creativity, Miaoli, Taiwan
2017 Outstanding Alumni, 22nd Edition, National Hsinchu University of Education

Exhibitions:
2006 Asian Ceramic Delta (Tour Exhibition of Taiwan, Japan, and Korea), Gifu, Japan
2007 Memoirs of a Recycling Yard, Solo Exhibition, Yingge Ceramics Museum, Taipei County, Taipei, Taiwan
2007 Marine Farm, Solo Exhibition, Taipei National University of the Arts - Kuandu Museum of Fine Arts, Taipei, Taiwan
2008 "Art and Craft," Olympic Cultural Festival, Beijing Contemporary Taiwan Ceramic Art Exhibition, Joint Exhibition, National Art Museum of China (Beijing)
2008 Ocean Log, Solo Exhibition, Tao Hua Zhuo Gallery
2011 Stone, Kungfu, Dolls, Solo Exhibition, Contemporary Taiwan Ceramic Art Exhibition, Miaoli, Taiwan
2014 China International Gallery Exposition, China National Convention Center , Beijing, China
2015 Art Kaohsiung, Joint Exhibition, Kaohsiung, Taiwan
2015 Art Formosa, Joint Exhibition, Taichung, Taiwan
2016 Between Virtual and Actual, Elsa Art Gallery, Joint Exhibition, Taipei, Taiwan
2016 Unadorable League, Solo Exhibition, River Art Gallery, Miaoli, Taiwan

Awards:
2008 Recommendation Prize, Taiwan Ceramics Biennale
2008 First Prize, Miaoli Ceramics Contest
2009 First Prize, Innovation Category, The Sixth Taipei Ceramics Awards
2009 Huang Xi Award, 3-D Craft Category, The Tenth Huang Xi Art Exhibition, Changhua County
2009 Silver Award, The Second Taiwan Gold Teapot Prizes
2009 Excellence Award, Miaoli Ceramics Contest
2010 Nanying Award, Tainan Nanying Biennial
2011 Silver Award, The Third Taiwan Gold Teapot Prizes

泡茶人木

Brewing Cha Ren More

真

陣式一

砂紅 Sand Red

紅砂 Red Sand
15x9x10cm / 1995

段泥提樑 Duan Mud Handle

段泥 Duan Mud
13.5x11.5x10cm / 1996

滚石不生苔
Rolling Stone Gathers No
Moss

陶土 Clay
10x11.5x6.5cm / 1996

大地 The Land

陶土 Clay
19x10.5x14cm / 1996

百岳 Mountains

陶土 Clay
15x9.5x17.5cm / 1997

晨曦 Dawn

陶土 Clay
20x24x23.5cm / 1997

石頭與鐵釘
Stone and Nail

陶土 Clay
15x10x10cm / 1997

銅紅提樑 Red Copper Handle

陶土 Clay
11.5x11x5.5cm / 1998

茶葉末側把 Tea Stem Handle

陶土 Clay
13x10.5x6cm / 1998

岩礦 Rock

陶土 Clay
14x9x9cm / 1998

山景開片 Mountain Landscapes

陶土 Clay
11x7x9cm / 1998

小胡瓜 Small Cucumber

瓷土 Porcelain clay
13x8.5x8cm / 2000

鐵甲蟲武士 Knight of Armored Beetle

陶土 Clay
17x11x15cm / 2007

山城玫瑰（壺）
Rose of the Mountain
City (Pot)

陶土 Clay
11.5x7x8cm / 2007

玫瑰山城
Mountain City
of Rose

陶土 Clay
20x14x8cm / 2008

海洋側把
Ocean Handle

陶土 Clay
18.5x11x13cm / 2007

晚霞
Dusk

陶土 Clay
21x13.5x13cm / 2008

山影 Mountains Silhouette

陶土 Clay
15x7x10cm / 2009

黑岩 Black Rock

陶土 Clay
16x10x12cm / 2010

日蝕
Solar eclipse

陶土 Clay
21x13x15cm / 2010

海洋茶具組
Ocean Tea Set

陶土 Clay
21x13x15cm / 2010

米兔海洋螯
Rice Rabbit & Crayfish

陶土 Clay
14x9x7.5cm / 2013

黑潮
Kuroshio Current

陶土 Clay
14x11x11cm / 2014

柴燒側把
Wood-fired Handle

陶土 Clay
12.5x10x8cm / 2014

米兔
Rice Rabbit

陶土 Clay
15x9x12cm / 2014

美人紅
Red Beauty

陶土 Clay
11x7x7cm / 2017

柴燒甕紅
Wood-fired Red Pot

陶土 Clay
12x7.5x8.5cm / 2016

我們都是人
We are All Human

陶土 Clay
最大：7x7x25cm
最小：3x15x1cm / 2016

蟹謝儂 (一)
Crap-shaped Pot (1)

陶土、磁鐵 Clay and magnet
12x7.5x8.5cm / 2018

黑壺
Black Pot

陶土 Clay
18x11.5x10.5cm / 2019

水尾海洋茶具組
Shuiwei Ocean Tea Set

陶土 Clay
最大：21x13x8cm
最小：2x3x5cm / 2020

蟹謝儂（二）
Crap-shaped Pot (2)

陶土、磁鐵 Clay and magnet
23x14x22cm / 2020

兩支公仔在海邊
Two Dolls by the Seaside

陶土 Clay
左：8x6x17cm
右：12x8x17cm / 2020

貳

陣式二

玩具大聯盟

Big League of Toys

Array 2

快樂杯 Happy Cup

陶土、現成五金 Clay and found metals
20x16x23cm / 2006

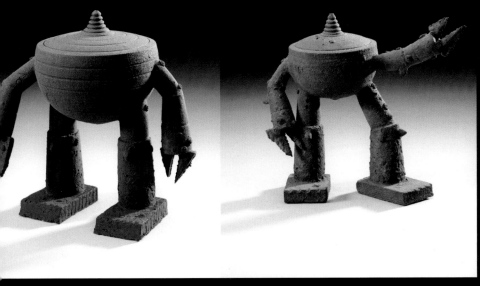

陀螺人
Top Person (Small)
Top Person (Large)

陶土 Clay
20x9x17cm（小）、 23x11x21.5cm（大）/ 2006

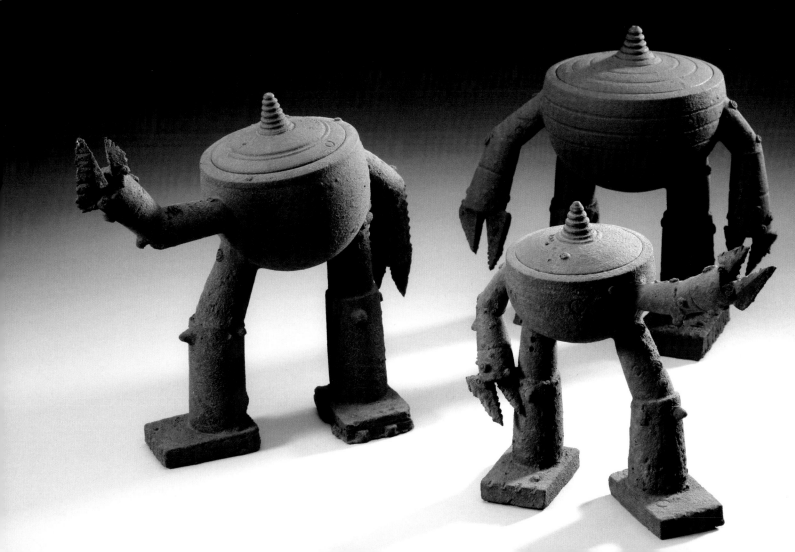

樂咖兄弟 (大) 樂咖兄弟 (小)
Happy Brothers (Large)
Happy Brothers (Small)

陶土、現成五金 Clay and found metals
25x11.5x27cm、19x10x24cm / 2007

飛天神兔
Flying Rabbit

陶土 Clay
27x16x29cm / 2007

候鳥使節
Migratory Bird Ambassador

陶土 Clay
25x11x22.5cm / 2007

蟲人
Worm Man

陶、琉璃、現成五金 Clay, glass and found metals
19x10.5x31cm / 2009

石怪
Stone Monster

陶土 Clay
7x7x13cm / 2009

魔人
Magic Cube

陶土、現成五金
Clay and found metals
9.5x4x15.5cm / 2009

加菲貓
Garfield the Cat

陶土 Clay
12x9.5x23cm / 2010

龍宮密使
Secret Envoy from the
Dragon Palace

陶土、現成五金 Clay and found metals
25x20x66cm / 2010

豬妳幸福
Piggy Wishes You Happy

陶土 Clay
31x32x57cm / 2011

石敢當創意技術學院（一）
Shi Gan Dang Creative College of
Technology (1)

陶土、現成五金 Clay and found metals
最大：29x20x17cm、最小：8x12x7cm / 2011

石敢當創意技術學院（二）
Shi Gan Dang Creative College of Technology (2)

陶土、現成五金 Clay and found metals
最大：29x20x17cm、最小：8x12x7cm / 2011

候鳥
Migratory Bird

陶土 Clay
34x20x67cm / 2011

鐵福龍
Tiefulong

陶土 Clay
26x23x31cm / 2012

金天牛
Golden Longicorn

陶土 Clay
22x17x30cm / 2012

悟空
Monkey King

陶土、現成五金 Clay and found metals
17x13x26cm / 2012

福虎生財
Fortune Tiger Brings Wealth

陶土 Clay
42x40x76cm / 2012

快樂獨角仙
Happy Rhinoceros Beetle

陶土 Clay
26x38x29cm / 2012

招財兔
Fortune Bringing Bunny

陶土 Clay
35x26x67cm / 2013

龍行守護者
Dragon Guard

陶土 Clay
30x26.5x50cm / 2013

藏蛇富
Fortune Snake

陶土 Clay
18x16x21cm / 2013

超馬
Super Horse

陶土 Clay
21x26x63cm / 2013

豬事如意
Piggy Brings Good Fortune

陶土 Clay
31x33x59cm / 2013

功夫（黑）
功夫（白）
Kung-fu (Black)
Kung-fu (White)

陶土 Clay
14x12x12、15x12x13cm / 2015

福臨人
Fortune Comes

陶土 Clay
15x8x27cm / 2015

畫唬人
Scary Person

陶土 Clay
9x8x18cm / 2015

勾勾纏
Twist

陶土 Clay
15x15x26cm / 2015

扮豬吃老虎
Pig in Disguise

陶土 Clay
30x31x60cm / 2015

萬磁小子
Magnetic Person

陶土 Clay
24x24x50cm / 2015

可愛聯盟
Cute League

陶土 Clay
不詳 / 2016

我流鼻血了
My Nose is Bleeding

陶土、現成五金、耐火磚
Clay, found metals, and refractory brick
11x5.5x29cm / 2016

情侶 (男)、情侶 (女)
Lovers (Man)、Lovers (Woman)

陶土 Clay
9.5x5x13cm / 2016

不想人
Not Thinking Person

陶土 Clay
9.5x8.5x25.5cm / 2016

快樂黑武士
Happy Dark Knight

陶土、現成五金 Clay and found metals
10.5x6x23cm / 2016

屌爆俠
Kick-Ass

陶土 Clay
21x12x31cm / 2016

值星官（生肖）
Duty Officer (Zodiac)

陶土 Clay
54x56x58cm / 2016

雞雞樂
Happy Chicken

陶土 Clay
63x49x81cm / 2016

霹靂鑽
Pili Drill

陶土 Clay
7x7x10.5cm / 2016

幸福栓
Happy Hydrant

陶土 Clay
32x22x82cm / 2016

大同寶寶
Tatung Doll

陶土 Clay
8x8x16cm / 2017

錢鼠錢
House Shrew

陶土 Clay
13x11x24cm / 2017

鋼鐵叮噹
Iron Cat

陶土 Clay
12.5x12x24.5cm / 2017

台灣囝仔
Taiwan Kid

陶土 Clay
11x11x17cm / 2017

遠古外星人
Antique Alien

陶土 Clay
19x9x21cm / 2017

超級戰士
Super Warrior

陶土 Clay
36x36x38cm / 2017

擁抱希望
Embrace Hope

陶土 Clay
65x34x104cm / 2018

超愛兔
Lovely Bunny

陶土 Clay
42x58x116cm / 2018

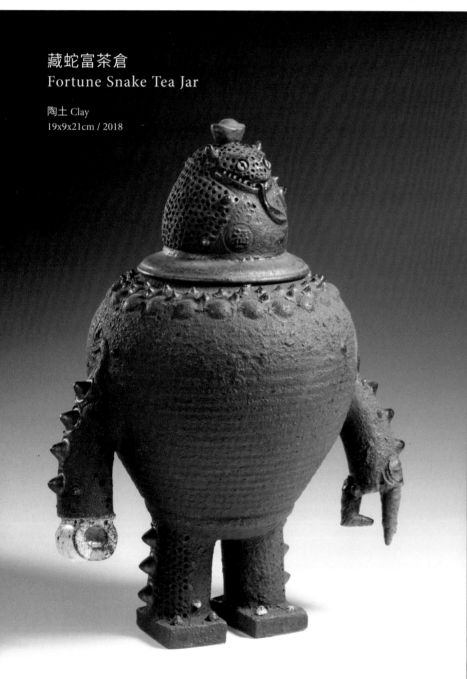

藏蛇富茶倉
Fortune Snake Tea Jar

陶土 Clay
19x9x21cm / 2018

看見 LOVE
See LOVE

陶土、燈組 Clay and lamp set
15x15x50cm / 2018

南瓜搗蛋鬼
Pumpkin Rascal

陶土、燈組 Clay and lamp set
10x11x31cm / 2018

葫蘆 D
Gourd D

陶土 Clay
39x35x103cm / 2018

寶寶愛抱抱
Baby Love Cuddling

陶土 Clay
43x29x52cm / 2019

兇案現場
Crime Scene

陶土 Clay
10x8x17cm / 2019

雙魚座女孩
Pisces Girl

陶土 Clay
14x12x29cm / 2019

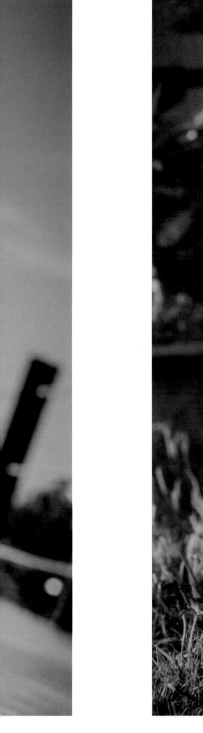

老公賺大錢
Hubby Makes Big Money

陶土 Clay
13x13x32cm / 2019

茶葉彈
Tea Bullet

陶土、培林 Clay and bearing
大：23x16x31cm、小：11x11x19cm / 2020

姐不是花瓶
I am not an ornament

陶土、培林 Clay and bearing
大：15x15x28cm、小：12x11x25cm / 2020

2020 防疫大作戰
2020 Big Anti-epidemic Warfare

陶土 Clay
33x17x44cm / 2020

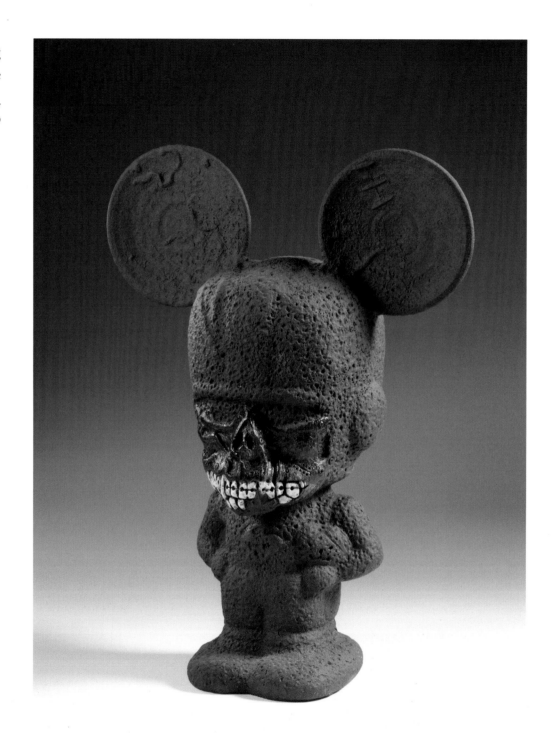

暴力米奇
Violent Mickey

陶土 Clay
21x16x38cm / 2020

鑄鐵鍋人
Cast Iron Pot Superman

陶土 Clay
17x16x25cm / 2020

暗黑 Ketty
Dark Ketty

陶土 Clay
14x12x19cm / 2020

奇幻海洋
Fantasy Ocean

陣式三

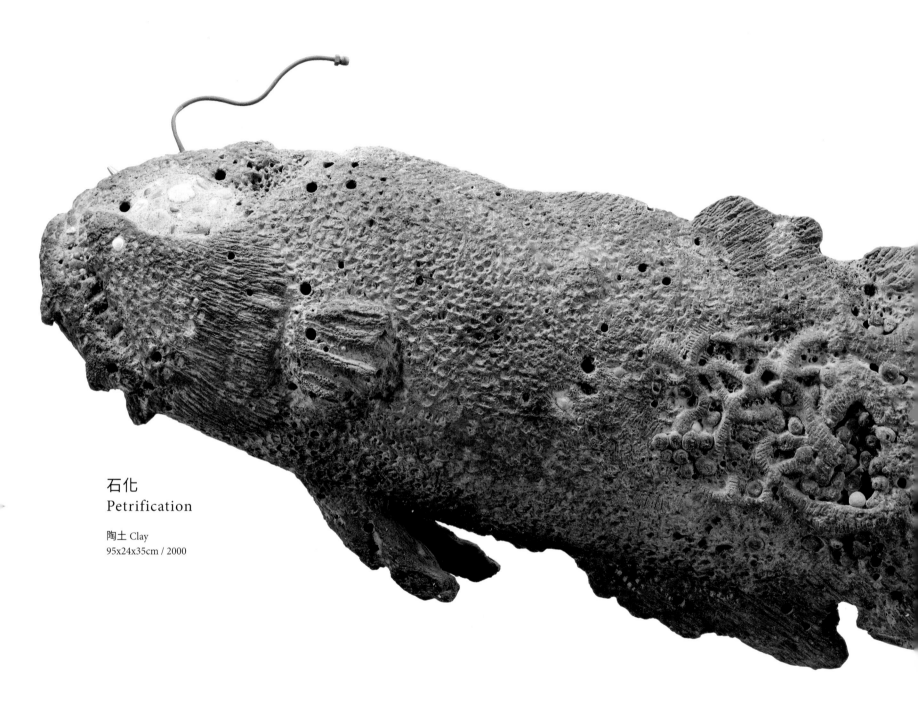

石化
Petrification

陶土 Clay
95x24x35cm / 2000

歸鄉
Home Coming

陶土、鐵條 Clay and iron bars
32x28x42cm / 2003

生命
Life

陶土 Clay
28x15x21cm / 2003

晚餐
Dinner

陶土 Clay
29x29x23cm / 2003

海洋（一）
Ocean (1)

陶土 Clay
53x30x40cm / 2004

海洋（二）
Ocean (2)

陶土 Clay
53x49x47cm / 2004

蟹蟹
Crab

陶土 Clay
27x22x12.2cm / 2004

海洋系列 -1 風華
Ocean Series – 1 Charm

陶土 Clay
45x36x41cm / 2004

海洋系列 -2 歲月
Ocean Series – 2 Time

陶土 Clay
28x21x27cm / 2005

海洋系列 -3 海洋情事
Ocean Series – 3 Ocean Affairs

陶土 Clay
81x33x58cm / 2005

碗蟹
Bowl Crab

陶土 Clay
52x46x34cm / 2005

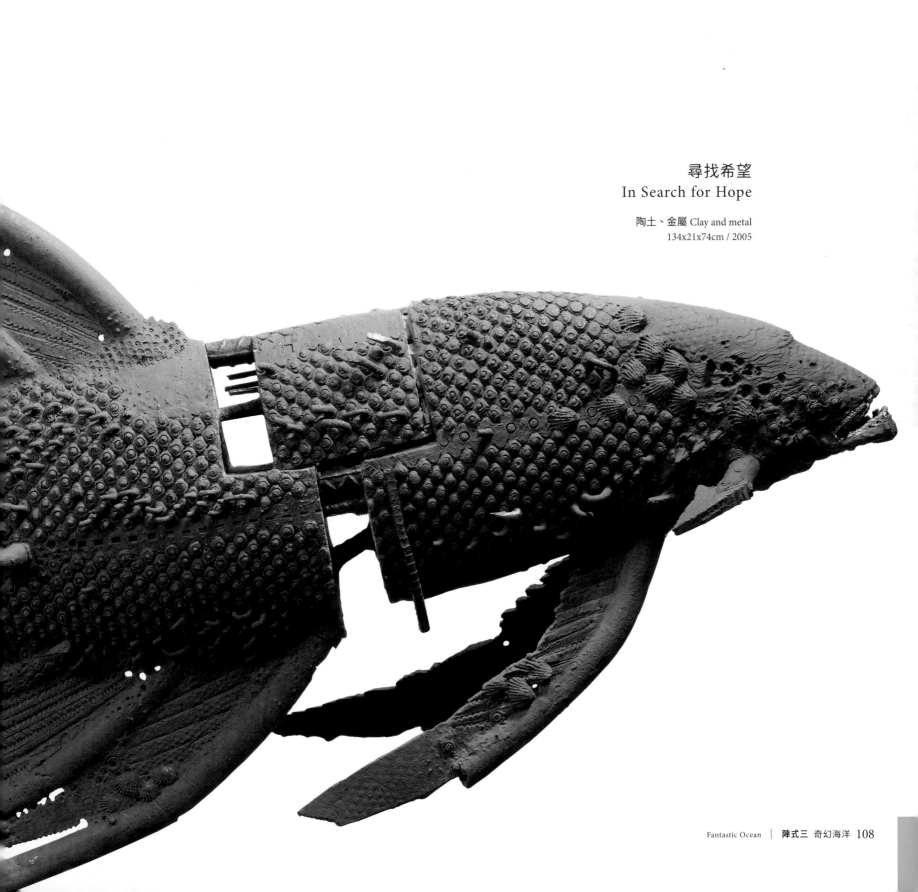

尋找希望
In Search for Hope

陶土、金屬 Clay and metal
134x21x74cm / 2005

望海
Sea Gazing

陶土 Clay
18x15x10cm / 2005

錦鯉
Koi

陶土 Clay
16x20x11cm / 2005

共生
Symbiosis

陶土 Clay
27x31x29cm / 2007

蝴蝶魚
Butterflyfish

陶土、鐵絲
Clay and iron wire
26x20x45cm / 2006

海洋記事
Ocean Log

陶土、鐵絲 Clay
最大：26x12x9cm、最小：1x1x2cm / 2007

殘存（一）
Remain (1)

陶土 Clay
16x6x7cm / 2007（單一，共 15 件）

殘存（二）
Remain (2)

陶土 Clay
65x39x41cm / 2008

殘存（三）
Remain (3)

陶土 Clay
67x39x39cm / 2008

海洋筆記本（一）
Ocean Notebook (1)

陶土 Clay
最大：24x18x23cm / 2008

海洋筆記本（二）
Ocean Notebook (2)

陶土、玻璃瓶 Clay and glass bottle
最大：25x18x16cm、最小：1x1x1cm / 2009

海洋筆記本（三）
Ocean Notebook (3)

陶土、玻璃瓶 Clay and glass bottle
最大：25x18x16cm、最小：1x1x1cm / 2009

殘存的氣息（一）
Last Breath (1)

陶土 Clay
40x24x29cm / 2009

殘存的氣息（二）
Last Breath (2)

陶土 Clay
32x18x15cm(單一) / 2007

海洋死亡帶
Ocean's Death Belt

陶土 Clay
最大：67x39x39cm、最小：1x1x0.5cm / 2009

擬態
Mimicry

陶土 Clay
42x30x18cm / 2014

海洋紀事
Ocean Memoir

陶土 Clay
62x124x55cm / 2014

魚躍龍門
Fish Leapt Over the
Dragon Gate

陶土 Clay
78x49x50m / 2014

進化
Evolution

陶土 Clay
50x63x65cm / 2014

鴻運當頭
Good Luck Comes

陶土 Clay
51x65x66cm / 2014

海洋記事
Ocean Log

複合媒材 Mixed media
最大：41x45x12cm、最小：1x3x3cm / 2020

肆

陣式四

天馬行空異質戀

Liberal Heterogenous Love

Array 4

水滴、墨壺、紙鎮筆架
Waterdrop, Inkpot, Paper Weight and Brush Rack

陶土、鋼管 Clay and steel pipe 、陶土、鋼管、木料 Clay, steel pipe, and wood 、陶土 Clay
7x7x5.5cm、8x8x12.5cm、14x9x8cm / 2014

訊息
Message

陶土、現成五金、燈組
Clay, found metals, and lamp set
17x17x32cm / 2006

帝寶
Dibao

陶土 Clay
10.5x10.5x62cm / 2006

香爐
Incense Burner

陶土、琉璃珠 Clay and glass beads
10x10x7.5cm / 2008

馬上賺
Instant Profit

不銹鋼、黑鐵
Stainless steel and black iron
14x10x26cm
限量 5/8 / 2014

超級英雄
Superhero

不銹鋼、銅
Stainless steel and copper
36x36x38cm
限量 2/8 / 2015

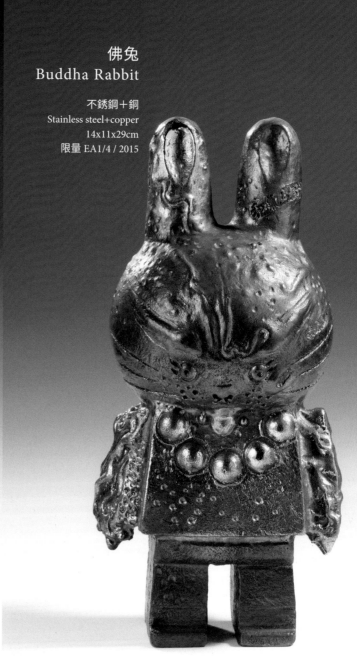

佛兔
Buddha Rabbit

不銹鋼＋銅
Stainless steel+copper
14x11x29cm
限量 EA1/4 / 2015

鐵工廠奇幻
Fantasy of an Iron
Factory

陶土 Clay
86x32x34cm /2016

獵殺狂派
Hunteroid

陶土、鐵 Clay and iron
32x22x69cm / 2016

青藏小子
Qingzang Kid

陶土、石頭 Clay and stone
13x6x14.5cm /2016

小掛心
Small Cabinet

陶土、木箱、現成五金
Clay, crates, and found metals
15x14x35cm /2016

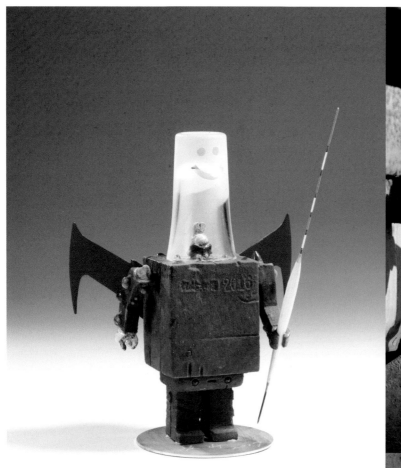

17 去釣魚
Go Fishing Together

陶土、玻璃杯 Clay and glass
11x6x20cm /2016

砲小子
Cannon Kid

陶土、現成五金、現成酒瓶
Clay, found metals, and found wine bottles
12x6x16cm /2018

照亮人
Light Person

陶土、現成五金、燈組
Clay, found metals, and lamp set
12x8x18cm /2018

小老頭(竹茶匙頭)
Little Old Man
(Bamboo Teaspoon)

複合媒材 Mixed media
8.5x7x20cm /2018

記憶人
Memory Person

陶土、玻璃皿 Clay and glass vessel
9.5x9.5x15cm /2016

對流人
Convection Person

陶土、金屬對流扇
Clay and metal convection fan
20x20x28cm /2019

屎爆俠
Kick-Ass

陶土 Clay
21x12x31m /2016

一卡箱仔
A Briefcase

陶土、玩具 Clay and toy
12x8x12cm /2019

使節
Diplomat

不鏽鋼 Stainless steel
23x15x28cm
限量 EA1/4 /2016

鹽晶人
Salt Crystal Person

陶土、鹽燈 Clay and salt lamp
19x12x22cm /2019

監測者 2019
Monitor 2019

陶土、現成五金
Clay and found metals
32x32x76cm /2019

終極陶陣

張山 創作展 CHANG Shan

109年苗栗縣美術家邀請展

主辦單位 / 苗栗縣政府

承辦單位 / 苗栗縣政府文化觀光局

發 行 人 / 徐耀昌

總 編 輯 / 林彥甫

編輯委員 / 王浩中、謝國昌、巫宇軒、劉慧珠

行政人員 / 曾新士、蕭雅文、周友蓮、李賢正

出版單位 / 苗栗縣政府文化觀光局

地　　址 / 苗栗市自治路50號

電　　話 / 037-352961

承印廠商 / 文森廣告實業社

地　　址 / 新竹市東區明湖里明湖路1243巷16號1樓

電　　話 / 03-5200852

出版日期 / 109年12月

定　　價 / 新台幣500元整

G　P　N / 1010901878

國家圖書館出版品預行編目(CIP)資料

109年苗栗縣美術家邀請展「終極陶陣 張山創作展」
2020/ 林彥甫總編輯.――苗栗市：苗縣文化觀光局, 民109.12
　　　面；　26x25 公分
ISBN 978-986-5420-60-4(平裝)
1.陶瓷工藝 2.作品集

938　　　　　　109018582